FULL COLOR
CAPTAIN UNDERPANTS
Double-Crunchy
BOOK O' FUN

DAV PILKEY

with color by Jose Garibaldi and Wes Dzioba

Scholastic Inc.

Library of Congress Control Number: 2021949400

ISBN 978-1-338-81449-1

10 9 8 7 6 5 4 3 2 1   22 23 24 25 26

Cover design by Dav Pilkey and Phil Falco
Book design by Dav Pilkey, Kathleen Westray, and Phil Falco
Color by Jose Garibaldi and Wes Dzioba

Printed in Mexico   188
First edition, November 2022

George and Harold's College O' Art

PAY ATTENTION NOW--- This will be on The Test!

WE'LL USE CAPTAIN UNDERPANTS AS OUR good guy.

Now we have to Think up A bAd guy.

HOW ABOUT A big, hAiRY ToiLeT WiTH WEREWOLF fangS?

HA-HA. OK!

Now THAT we've got OUR bad guy, WE Need To KNOW ALL About him... WHAT POWERS does he hAVE? How did he become So EViL?

LASER BeAM

KUNG-Fu GRiP

P.U.

STiNKY FeeT

Atomic ButT

NUCLEAR WASTe is oFten To blAme foR CREATiNG eviL MONSTERS. IT's The comic BooK MAKER'S BeST fRiENd!

NEW CLEAR WASTE

NOW WE NEED A STORY, SO LET YOUR IMAGINATION RUN WILD! THIS REQUIRES LOTS OF DAYDREAMING!

DAYDREAMING IS FUN, AND YOU CAN DO IT ALMOST ANYWHERE--IN CLASS, ON THE BUS, OR EVEN AT HOME!

DAYDREAMERS AT WORK! -DO NOT DISTURB!!

EDITOR'S NOTE: YOU really shouldn't daydream in class!

ANOTHER GREAT WAY TO THINK UP STORIES IS CALLED "BRAINSTORMING." THIS IS WHERE YOU GET TOGETHER WITH A FRIEND AND LET THE IDEAS FLY!

LET'S MAKE HIS ARMS AND LEGS REA... SO WHE... FALLS...

His LASER BEAMS Should be REALLY... So when CAPTAIN...

We Should MAKE it LiKE THAT MOVIE About THE DINOSAURS.

YOU MEAN "TITANIC"?

.. BUT THAT WHAT ENDS...

Oh YEAH! WE CAN TELL THE...

NO! THE ONE WITH THE big T. REX!

"IT'S A WONDERFUL LIFE"?

HA-HA-HA HA-HA!!

HA-HA HA-HA!

That's it!

Then we c... The ending CHANGES...

Then YOU DRAW his FALLING!

YEAH!

REMEMBER: TWO BRAINS ARE OFTEN BETTER THAN ONE!

When you've figured out your story, you can start drawing your comic. This is where TEAMWORK comes in handy. I do ALL The WRITING 'cause I'm a good speller...

...And I do ALL The drawing because I'm A good ARTiST!

Don't WORRY if you make MISTAKES --- it happens To The best of us.

That's why They invenTed ERASERS.

RUB RUB RUB

Now JUST keep WRITING And dRAWING UnTiL you've finished Telling your STORY.

MANY COMIC BOOKS END WITH A BIG FIGHT. IF YOU HAVE TROUBLE WRITING ACTION SCENES, YOU CAN ALWAYS USE FLIP-O-RAMA INSTEAD.

TURN TO PAGE 22 TO LEARN HOW TO MAKE YOUR VERY OWN FLIP-O-RAMAS.

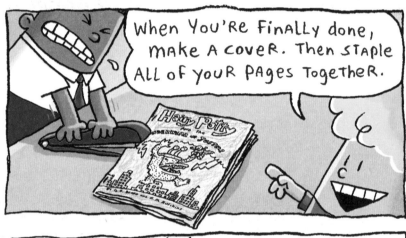

WHEN YOU'RE FINALLY DONE, MAKE A COVER. THEN STAPLE ALL OF YOUR PAGES TOGETHER.

TA-DAAA! YOUR VERY OWN COMIC BOOK!

NOW GO MAKE COPIES OF IT AND SELL THEM ON THE PLAYGROUND!!!

PROFESSOR POOPYPANTS'S PREPOSTEROUS PUZZLES OF PERPLEXING PERIL PART 1

Hello kiddies! I've taken my terrifying Name Change-o-Chart 2000 and turned it into a WORD FIND PUZZLE! Try to find all the names from the chart below in the puzzle on the right. Look up, down, across, and backward!

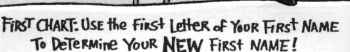

1

FIRST CHART: USE the First Letter of YOUR First NAME To DeTermine YOUR NEW First NAME!

A = Stinky
B = Lumpy
C = Buttercup
D = Gidget
E = Crusty
F = Greasy
G = Fluffy
H = Cheeseball
I = Chim-Chim

J = Poopsie
K = Flunky
L = Booger
M = Pinky
N = Zippy
O = Goober
P = Doofus
Q = Slimy

R = Loopy
S = Snotty
T = Falafel
U = Dorky
V = Squeezit
W = Oprah
X = Skipper
Y = Dinky
Z = Zsa-Zsa

L	U	M	P	Y	U	M	T	E	Y
L	O	O	P	Y	S	I	C	I	K
A	S	Z	A	S	Z	H	R	S	N
B	U	T	T	E	R	C	U	P	I
E	H	S	L	R	J	M	S	O	D
S	Q	U	E	E	Z	I	T	O	G
E	Y	F	F	P	I	H	Y	P	R
E	F	O	A	P	P	C	F	R	E
H	F	O	L	I	P	L	L	A	A
C	U	D	A	K	Y	G	U	H	S
I	L	G	F	S	T	I	N	K	Y
F	F	Y	K	R	O	D	K	V	M
S	N	P	B	L	M	G	Y	D	I
R	E	B	O	O	G	E	R	L	L
P	I	N	K	Y	T	T	O	N	S

(Answer on page 120)

HOW TO DRAW
CAPTAIN UNDERPANTS

1.

2.

3.

4.

5.

6.

7.

8.

9.

10.

11.

12.

13.

14.

15.

16.

CAN YOU ESCAPE DOCTOR DIAPER'S DEVASTATING DIAPER OF DOOM?

(Answer on page 120)

14

"Knock knock?"
"Who's there?"
"I'm a pileup."
"I'm a pileup who?"
"No, you're not! Don't be so hard on yourself, buddy!"

Q) What did the momma buffalo say to the baby buffalo when he went off to college?
A) Bison.

Q) What does lightning wear beneath its clothes?
A) Thunderwear.

Q) What should you do if you get swallowed by an elephant?
A) Jump up and down 'til you're all pooped out.

Q) Why did Batman cross his legs?
A) He had to go to the batroom.

Q) If you had fifty bananas in one hand, and twenty-five gallons of ice cream in the other, what would you have?
A) Really big hands.

THE PERILOUS PUZZLE OF PROFESSOR POOPYPANTS

ACROSS

2. The alien spacemen were named Zorx, Klax, and _____.

4. Harold's best friend is _____.

5. "George is the kid on the left with the _____ and the flat-top."

7. George's best friend is _____.

8. Don't get "weeded out" by the Deliriously Dangerous Death-Defying _____ of Doom.

10. Dr. Diaper wanted to blow up the _____.

12. Captain Underpants is also known as a principal named Mr. _____.

14. Don't get flushed by the Turbo _____ 2000!

15. "Yum, _____, eat 'em up!"

DOWN

1. "Never underestimate the power of _____."

3. _____ Horwitz Elementary School

4. Don't get blown up by the Goosy- _____ 4000.

6. Ms. Ribble is George and Harold's _____.

7. "Harold is the one on the right with the T-shirt and the bad _____."

9. Captain Underpants fights crime with Wedgie _____.

11. Professor Poopypants's first name.

13. Don't get shrunk by the Shrinky-_____ 2000.

(Answer on page 121)

HOW TO DRAW
THE TURBO TOILET 2000

1.

2.

3.

4.

5.

6.

7.

8.

9.

10.

11.

12.

13.

14.

15.

16.

PROFESSOR POOPYPANTS'S
PREPOSTEROUS PUZZLES
OF PERPLEXING PERIL
PART 2

So you solved my last puzzle, eh? Well, don't get too full of yourself. This puzzle is <u>much</u> <u>harder</u>—it's got DIAGONALS! Try to find all the names from the chart below in the puzzle on the right. Look up, down, across, <u>diagonal</u>, and backward!

2

SECOND CHART: USE the first letter of your LAST NAME to determine the FIRST half of your **NEW** Last Name.

A = Diaper
B = Toilet
C = Giggle
D = Bubble
E = Girdle
F = Barf
G = Lizard
H = Waffle
I = Cootie

J = Monkey
K = Potty
L = Liver
M = Banana
N = Rhino
O = Burger
P = Hamster
Q = Toad

R = Gizzard
S = Pizza
T = Gerbil
U = Chicken
V = Pickle
W = Chuckle
X = Tofu
Y = Gorilla
Z = Stinker

C	H	I	C	K	E	N	O	D	I	C	D
B	J	B	U	B	B	L	E	T	O	F	U
D	R	A	Z	Z	I	G	K	O	N	D	Q
L	G	E	X	N	O	I	T	C	C	R	B
A	I	D	T	R	M	I	O	I	U	R	I
N	G	Z	I	S	E	A	V	P	D	H	E
A	G	L	A	A	M	K	P	T	A	I	C
N	L	G	G	R	P	A	N	O	O	N	T
A	E	I	I	E	D	E	H	I	T	O	L
B	U	R	G	E	R	D	R	L	T	T	O
K	J	D	F	R	A	B	O	E	V	S	Y
G	E	L	K	C	I	P	I	T	V	V	R
G	Y	E	K	N	O	M	R	L	U	I	X
W	A	F	F	L	E	P	I	Z	Z	A	L

(Answer on page 121)

21

George And Harold's College O' Art 2

MAKE YOUR OWN FLIP-O-RAMA!!!

BECAUSE MOST PAPER is A LITTLE TRANSPARENT, YOU SHOULD STILL KINDA BE ABLE TO SEE YOUR DRAWING UNDERNEATH.

I CAN KINDA SEE IT!

IF YOU CAN'T SEE YOUR DRAWING UNDERNEATH THE TOP SHEET OF PAPER, JUST HOLD IT UP TO A SUNNY WINDOW.

COOL!

NOW WE'RE GOING TO DO SOME TRACING ON THE TOP PAGE. THE **1**ST RULE IS:

IF YOU <u>DON'T</u> WANT SOMETHING TO MOVE, **TRACE IT!!!**

And since he's dribbling the ball on the floor, I'll redraw the ball down on the floor.

Harold has just shown the **2ND** rule of FLIP-O-RAMA: If you want something to move, you must **REDRAW** it in a <u>new</u> <u>position</u>.

 Look at Harold's two drawings below... Notice the differences.

FIRST DRAWING (BOTTOM PAGE)	SECOND DRAWING (TOP PAGE)

Soon you cAn move on to more exciting FLiP-O-RAMAs, Like Kicks, Punches, And heAd injuries!

You'LL be A FLiP-O-RAMA MASTeR, with The power to AmAZe And delight every-one you meeT.

...WeLL, ALMost everyone!

HAPPY FLiPPiNG

Hey KidS--- Check out the WorLD's EASIEST FLiP-O-RAMA!!!

Right
index
Finger
Here

☆ SPECIAL NOTES ☆
FOR FLIP-O-RAMISTS

1. Typing paper and notebook paper work best.

2. Although you need to trace, don't use tracing paper. It will ruin the effect.

3. Grown-ups will freak out if your flip-o-Ramas feature "people" beating each other up. To get around this, draw robots and monsters instead. (For some REASON, Grown-ups think that's o.k. ...Go Figure!)

4. You can get good ideas by studying the FLIP-O-RamAS in The CAptain UNderpants and Dog Man Books.

Q) Why do sharks live in salt water?
A) Because pepper water makes them sneeze.

Q) How do you make a tissue dance?
A) Put a little boogie into it.

Q) Why did Tigger stick his head in the toilet?
A) He was looking for "Pooh."

Q) Who is Peter Pan's worst-smelling friend?
A) Stinkerbell.

Q) What nationality are you when you go to the bathroom?
A) European.

A woman walks into a pet store and says, "Can I get a puppy for my daughter?"
"Sorry, lady," says the pet store owner. "We don't do trades."

HOW TO DRAW
PROFESSOR POOPYPANTS

1. 2. 3. 4.

5. 6. 7.

8. 9.

10.

36

THE CAFETERIA LADIES' CRAZY CROSSWORD

ACROSS

  1. *The Adventures of* _____ *Underpants.*

  5. Mr. Krupp was transformed into a superhero by the 3-D Hypno-_____.

  6. Watch out for the Equally Evil Lunchroom _____ Nerds.

  8. Pippy P. Poopypants invented the _____ Jogger 2000.

10. "Hooray for Captain _____!"

11. Don't drink the Evil Zombie Nerd _____!

13. Captain Underpants often shouts "_____-La-Laaaaa!"

14. *Cheesy Animation Technology* is more commonly known as _____-O-Rama.

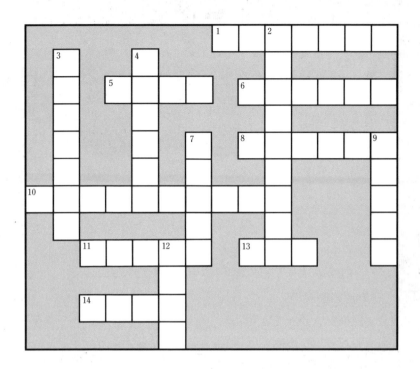

DOWN

2. *The Perilous Plot of _____ Poopypants.*

3. *The Attack of the _____ Toilets.*

4. Dr. _____ was defeated soon after George shot fake doggy doo-doo at him.

7. Zorx, Klax, and Jennifer were evil guys from outer _____.

9. A popular way to misspell the word "laughs."

12. Captain Underpants wears a red _____.

(Answer on page 121)

PROFESSOR POOPYPANTS'S PREPOSTEROUS PUZZLES OF PERPLEXING PERIL PART 3

Now comes the hardest puzzle of all. If you mess this one up, you must use the three Name Change-o-Chart 2000 charts to change your name FOREVER! Try to find all the names from the chart below in the puzzle on the right. Look up, down, across, <u>diagonal</u>, and backward!

3

Third Chart: Use the last letter of your last name to determine the second half of your NEW last name.

A = Head
B = Mouth
C = Face
D = Nose
E = Tush
F = Breath
G = Pants
H = Shorts
I = Lips

J = Honker
K = Butt
L = Brain
M = Tushie
N = Chunks
O = Hiney
P = Biscuits
Q = Toes

R = Buns
S = Fanny
T = Sniffer
U = Sprinkles
V = Kisser
W = Squirt
X = Humperdinck
Y = Brains
Z = Juice

```
H  S  T  I  U  C  S  I  B  G  H
U  P  E  S  K  N  U  H  C  E  T
M  I  R  L  I  O  Y  U  A  H  U
P  L  J  A  K  P  E  D  S  S  O
E  V  R  Q  O  N  N  N  J  H  M
R  B  V  S  Q  U  I  R  T  O  Q
D  Q  M  W  S  F  H  R  Q  R  F
I  H  A  G  F  A  N  E  P  T  Q
N  B  R  E  A  T  H  I  F  S  P
C  M  R  E  K  N  O  H  A  R  F
K  S  S  F  S  O  J  S  N  R  N
J  P  A  N  T  S  U  U  N  G  B
J  C  L  O  U  E  I  T  Y  B  U
E  D  Y  E  S  B  C  K  D  W  T
Q  U  E  F  H  S  E  O  T  V  T
```

(Answer on page 122)

WELCOME TO A BRAND-NEW CAPTAIN UNDERPANTS STORY . . . AND YOU'RE THE STAR!

Before you read the story on the following pages, go through and find all the blanks. Below each blank is a small description of what you need to write in the blank. Just fill in the blank with an appropriate word.

For example, if the blank looks like this:

_____ , you would think up an adjective
(an adjective)

and put it in the blank like this: _____Stinky_____ .
(an adjective)

Remember, don't read the story first. It's more fun if you go through and fill in the blanks first, THEN read the story.

When you're done, follow the instructions at the bottom of each page to complete the illustrations. Cool, huh?

JUST FOR REMINDERS:

A **verb** is an <u>action</u> word (like jump, swim, kick, squish, run, etc.).
An **adjective** is a word that <u>describes</u> a person, place, or thing (lumpy, purple, hairy, etc.).

CAPTAIN UNDERPANTS VS.
THE EVIL MONSTER
(STARRING GEORGE, HAROLD, AND YOU!)

Once upon a time, George, Harold, and their

friend _____ were busy studying
　　　　　　(your name)

about the wonders of _____
　　　　　　　　　　　　　　(an adjective)

_____ , when their new science
(disgusting things)

teacher, Mr. _____ , accidentally
　　　　　　　　(a funny name)

spilled some _____ _____
　　　　　　　(a gross adjective)　　　　(a liquid)

on a pile of toxic _____ .
　　　　　　　　　　(silly things)

↑ (Draw yourself
sitting here.)

↖ (Draw the teacher spilling
liquid onto some toxic stuff.)

43

Suddenly, the pile began to morph into

a giant, evil _____ .
          (a silly thing)

   "Help," cried _____ , "a
                (somebody in your class)

giant, evil _____
          (the silly thing you just used above)

just stepped on my lunchbox and ate up

_____ !"
(your gym teacher's name)

   "Oh, NO!" cried Mr. Krupp. "The poor

lunchbox!"

↑   ↖
(Draw the giant,   (Draw the kid
 evil monster.)   in your class.)

George, Harold, and _____
(your name)

tried to escape by hiding behind a

_____ . Then _____
(a very small thing)   (your name)

snapped _____ fingers.
(his/her/their/etc.)

Soon, a _____ grin came
(an adjective)

across Mr. Krupp's face as he dropped

his _____ _____
(an adjective)   (an article of clothing)

and ran to his office.

↑ (Draw yourself.)   ↑ (Draw the thing you're hiding behind.)   ↖ (Draw the giant, evil monster.)

Soon, Captain Underpants

_____ through the
(an action verb ending in "ed")

wall. He grabbed a _____
(an adjective)

_____ and hit the monster
(a thing)

on its _____ .
(a body part)

"Ouchies!" screamed the monster. It

turned and _____
(a fight move ending in "ed")

Captain Underpants on his

_____ .
(a body part)

(Draw ↑
yourself.)

↖
(Draw the monster fighting
Captain Underpants.)

_____ quickly mixed up a bottle
(your name)

of _____ with a jar of toxic,
(something a kid would drink)

_____ _____ .
(an adjective)   (disgusting things)

"Hey, _____ ," said George,
(your name)

"where'd you find that jar of crazy stuff?!!?"

"It was right here next to this barrel of

toxic _____ _____ ," said
(an adjective)   (different disgusting things)

_____ .
(your name)

"Oh," said Harold. "That makes sense."

↑
(Draw yourself creating
a strange mixture.)

↑
(Complete the label
on the barrel.)

47

_____ shook up the strange

(your name)

mixture and threw it at the monster.

"_____ !" screamed

(something you might scream or cheer)

the monster as it fell over and died

of a massive _____ attack.

(a body part)

"That makes sense, too," said George.

Unfortunately, some of the mixture

splashed on Captain Underpants's head,

and he turned back into Mr. Krupp.

(Draw yourself throwing the strange
concoction onto the monster.)

(Draw the monster
getting splashed.)

"HOLY _____ _____ !"
(an adjective)   (silly animals)

shouted Mr. Krupp. "I'll bet that George,

Harold, and _____ are responsible
(your name)

for this mess!" So he punished the three kids

by making them _____ in the
(an action verb)

_____ for _____ hours.
(a room in the school)   (a number)

     "This has got to be the dumbest story

we've ever been in," said George.

     "Don't blame me," said Harold. "_____
(your name)

wrote it!"

↑
(Draw yourself
looking guilty.)

ZORX, KLAX, AND Jennifer's Big, BAD BATCH OF ZOMBIE NERD Juice

OPEN

Lunar Farms ★ ZOMBIE ★ NERD JUICE

ULTRA-PASTEURIZED

(Answer on page 122)

FINAL EXAM

Hi everybody!
One thing I know for sure is that kids LOVE to study and take tests! That's why we've included this incredibly difficult FINAL EXAM! Make sure you've studied BOTH of George and Harold's College o' Art comics. When you think you're ready, take out a pencil, turn the page, and begin.
Good Luck!

1. What's the BEST way to think up a story?
a) Create characters.
b) Put a grilled cheese sandwich on your head.
c) Roll around in steak sauce, then bark like a dog.

2. What is often to blame for creating monsters?
a) society
b) pep rallies
c) nuclear waste

3. What two things also help you think up stories?
a) brainstorming and daydreaming
b) braindreaming and daystorming
c) daybraining and dreamstorming

4. Don't worry about making mistakes. That's why they invented _____.
a) lawyers
b) erasers
c) soap-on-a-rope

5. If you have trouble writing action scenes, you can always use _____.
a) a ghost writer
b) Flip-O-Rama
c) egg salad

6. When making comics, be prepared to:
a) win friends and influence people
b) smell like Cheez Whiz™
c) suffer for your art

7. What's the world's EASIEST Flip-O-Rama?
a) a guy with a chicken up his nose
b) a guy with a basketball
c) a guy with a basketball up his nose

8. The FIRST rule of Flip-O-Rama is: If you don't want something to move, _____.
a) trace it
b) put it in a "time-out"
c) threaten to stop the car

9. The SECOND rule of Flip-O-Rama is: If you want something to move, you must _____.
a) make rude noises with your armpits
b) drink lots of prune juice
c) redraw it in a new position

10. The more you practice, _____.
a) the better you get
b) the worse you get
c) the stinkier you get

Now put your pencil down, and let's see how you did.

ANSWERS:
1: a, 2: c (though technically "b" is also correct),
3: a, 4: b, 5: b, 6: c, 7: b, 8: a, 9: c, 10: a

If you got at least 6 right, CONGRATULATIONS! You've just graduated from George and Harold's College o' Art.

(Answer on page 123)

Hairy Potty
AND the
UNDERWEAR of JUSTICE

BY G. R. BEARD and H.M. Hutchins

Once upon a time There was a scientist who worked At "Hair Group for Guys."

HAIR GROUP LABORAT

He was trying To invent a Hair Growth Formula.

Hmmm.

But it didn't work.

Fooey!

Then he tried Adding **NUCLEAR WASTE** To his concoction.

The scientist decided to get rid of the bad formula so that nothing else would grow big and hairy and evil.

So he poured it down the toilet.

Bye-bye, evil formula.

BUT---He forgot to FLUSH!

La-La-La-La.

Soon, the toilet grew hair.

Then the Toilet grew BIG.

Dum-de Dum.

Then the toilet grew evil!

Uh-oh!

RAAAAAR!

BONK

owie!

The scientist Reached FOR A can of "POTTY-BE-GONE" Brand Toilet Remover...

...but the box WAS empty!

POTTY-BE GONE
TOILET REMOVE

Time TO RE-ORDER

TERMINATE YOUR TOILET!

GuLp.

The HAIRY Potty Shot a LASER BEAM From his Mouth And **ZAPPED** the scientist.

AW, MAN!

Hairy Potty Shot His Laser And made A Hole in the Wall.

ZAP

I'm FREE!!!

Then He RAN AROUND CAUSING Mischief.

BOB'S DINER
AT BOB'S DINER, You'll Find That We Pick The BEST ingredients. Your Nose KNOWS The difference!
Hmmm.

ZAP

BOB'S
AT BOB'S DINER, We Pick Your Nose
HAW HAW HAW

Then HAIRY POTTY RAN To A school.
LA-LA LA-LA.

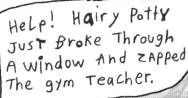

Help! Hairy Potty Just Broke Through A window And Zapped The gym Teacher.

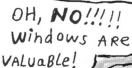

OH, **NO**!!!!! Windows Are VALUABLE!

This Looks Like A Job For...

...CAPTAIN UNDERPANTS!

CRASH

What seems to be the Problem, Bub?

HAiRY POttY!

UH-OH!

THUMP THUMP THUMP

To be continued . . .

WEDGIE-POWERED WORD FIND

Try to find the names below in the puzzle on the right. Look up, down, backward, and diagonally.

CHARACTER NAME BONUS QUIZ:
How well do you know your UNDERPANTS?

Draw lines from the <u>first</u> names in Chart A to the matching <u>last</u> names in Chart B.

CHART A	CHART B
Benny	Beard
Billy	Fyde
George	Hoskins
Harold	Hutchins
Melvin	Krupp
Morty	Poopypants
Pippy	Ribble
Tara	Sneedly
Tippy	Tinkletrousers

```
S  T  N  A  P  Y  P  O  O  P
R  U  O  R  L  Y  H  Q  N  A
E  G  N  L  V  X  T  V  F  F
S  N  I  H  C  T  U  H  L  Z
U  B  V  M  A  L  O  E  S  A
O  A  L  F  O  S  G  D  R  J
R  U  E  C  K  R  R  A  Q  E
T  F  M  I  O  A  T  D  D  I
E  S  N  E  E  D  L  Y  V  E
L  S  G  B  L  O  F  L  R  S
K  Q  F  F  R  B  P  C  P  U
N  S  E  A  E  R  B  I  C  R
I  A  H  N  Y  P  P  I  T  Z
T  X  N  M  J  P  P  U  R  K
K  Y  Q  B  Y  R  Z  X  D  C
```

(Answers on page 123)

HOW TO DRAW
CAPTAIN UNDERPANTS

1.
2.
3.
4.
5.
6.
7.
8.
9.
10.

PERPLEXING PEEWEE-POWERED PUZZLE

ACROSS

3. Captain Underpants fights for Truth, Justice, and all that is Pre-Shrunk and _____!

5. A flushable porcelain bowl.

7. "Tra-_____-Laaaaa!"

8. Super Diaper Baby's archenemy is _____ Doo-Doo.

9. Captain Underpants is nicknamed the _____ Warrior.

10. Super Diaper Baby's best friend is Diaper _____.

11. The only five-letter word (starting with an "s") to appear twice in the last six clues.

14. Watch out for the Wicked Wedgie _____!

15. Liquid spray _____ is the enemy of underwear.

DOWN

1. The three evil space guys were named _____, Klax, and Jennifer.

2. New Swissland's most famous scientist is Professor _____.

3. Three cheers for _____ Underpants!

4. _____ Potty and the Underwear of Justice.

6. Beware of the _____ Toilet 2000!

10. Billy Hoskins is better known as Super _____ Baby.

12. Don't spill the Extra-Strength Super _____ Juice!

13. Ms. _____ turned into the Wicked Wedgie Woman.

(Answer on page 124)

HOW TO DRAW
MR. KRUPP

70

HeLP George and Harold GeT into Their TREE House

START HERE

END HERE

(Answer on page 125)

72

Q) Why did the cookie cry?
A) Because his mom had been a wafer so long.

"Knock knock."
"Who's there?"
"Olive Toop."
"Olive Toop who?"
"Well, so do I, but you don't hear me braggin' about it!"

Ms. Ribble: Harold, if I gave you two goldfish, and Melvin gave you four goldfish, how many would you have?
Harold: Eleven.
Ms. Ribble: ELEVEN?!!? Hah! You're WRONG, bub!
Harold: No, you're wrong. I already have five goldfish back at home!

Melvin: Excuse me, mister, I'd like to buy some toilet paper.
Grocery store clerk: What color would you like?
Melvin: Just give me white. I'll color it myself!

Q) What do you get when you cross a porcupine with a great white shark?
A) As far away as possible.

HOW TO DRAW
GEORGE

1.

2.

3.

4.

5.

6.

7.

8.

9.

10.

11.

12.

13.

14.

15.

16.

75

HOW TO DRAW
HAROLD

1.

2.

3.

4.

5.

6.

7.

8.

9.

10.

76

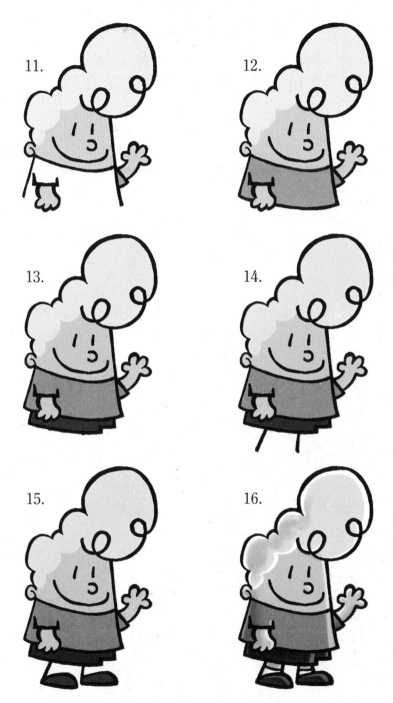

11.

12.

13.

14.

15.

16.

NOW YOU CAN BE THE STAR OF YOUR OWN SUPER-CHEESY CAPTAIN UNDERPANTS STORY!

Before you read the story on the following pages, go through and find all the blanks. Below each blank is a small description of what you need to write in the blank. Just fill in the blank with an appropriate word.

For example, if the blank looks like this:

_____ , you would think up an adjective
(an adjective)

and put it in the blank like this: ____Snotty____ .
(an adjective)

Remember, don't read the story first. It's more fun if you go through and fill in the blanks first, THEN read the story.

When you're done, follow the instructions at the bottom of each page to complete the illustrations. Cool, huh?

JUST FOR REMINDERS:
A **verb** is an <u>action</u> word (like jump, swim, kick, squish, run, etc.).
An **adjective** is a word that <u>describes</u> a person, place, or thing (lumpy, purple, hairy, etc.).

THE INCREDIBLY STUPID ADVENTURE OF CAPTAIN UNDERPANTS

This is George Beard, Harold Hutchins,

and _____ _____ .
           (your first name)   (your last name)

George is the one on the left with the tie and

the flat-top. Harold is the one on the right

with the T-shirt and the bad haircut.

_____ is the one in the middle
(your first name)

with the _____ _____
           (an adjective)   (article of clothing)

and the _____ _____ .
          (an adjective)   (body part or parts)

Remember that now.

↑
(Draw yourself here.)

79

One day, George, Harold, and _____
were at school when suddenly, an evil, _____
villain _____ through the door and
roared like a ferocious _____ .

"My name is Commander _____
_____ !" shouted the villain. "And I've come
to destroy all the _____ in the world!"

Commander _____
grabbed a _____ and started hitting
_____ on the _____ with it.

"Oh no!" cried _____ . "That villain is
going to hurt the poor _____ !"

(Draw yourself here.)   (Draw your evil villain here.)

"We've got to stop that monster!" cried

George. He reached into his _____ ,
(an article of clothing)

grabbed a/an _____ _____ ,
(an adjective)   (something big)

and threw it at the villain.

Harold found a/an _____ in his
(something bigger)

_____ , so he threw that, too. Finally,
(an article of clothing)

_____ reached into his/her/their_____ ,
(your name)   (an article of clothing)

pulled out a/an _____ _____ ,
(an adjective)   (the biggest thing you can think of)

and threw that as well.

But nothing seemed to stop the _____
(a disgusting adjective)

Commander _____ !
(the gross adjective and thing you used twice on page 80)

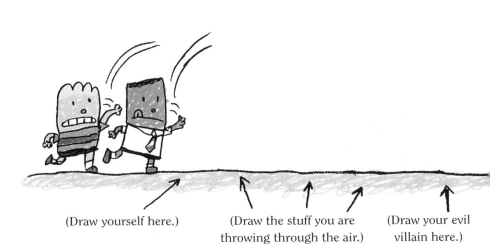

(Draw yourself here.)   (Draw the stuff you are   (Draw your evil
                              throwing through the air.)   villain here.)

"This looks like a job for Captain Underpants!"

shouted _____ .
(your first name)

Suddenly, Captain Underpants _____
(a verb ending in "ed")
into the school. "Hi," said Captain Underpants.

"How's your _____ _____
(an adjective) (an animal)
_____ today?"
(a part of the body)

"That doesn't make any sense," said Harold.

"Who cares?" said _____ . "We've got
(your first name)
to stop that villain!" So Captain Underpants

grabbed a baseball bat and hit Commander

_____ over the
(the gross adjective and thing you used twice on page 80)
head repeatedly.

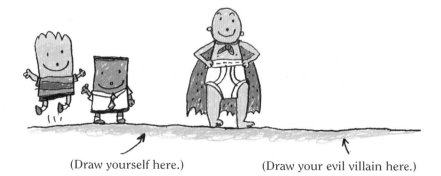

(Draw yourself here.)   (Draw your evil villain here.)

HERE COMES THE BAT, MAN!

(Draw your villain here. Make him about the same height
as Captain Underpants. If you need help, look at the
Flip-O-Ramas on pages 31 and 33 for inspiration.)

HERE COMES THE BAT, MAN!

(Draw your villain here. Make him about the same height as Captain Underpants. If you need help, look at the Flip-O-Ramas on pages 31 and 33 for inspiration.)

"Holy _____ _____ !" shouted
(a verb ending in "ing")   (an animal)

George. "Captain Underpants has defeated

Commander _____!"
(the gross adjective and thing you used twice on page 80)

"Let's celebrate by eating _____ servings of
(a number)

_____ _____ and drinking _____cups
(an adjective)   (something gross)   (a number)

of _____ _____ ," said Harold.
(an adjective)   (a disgusting liquid)

"That sounds delicious," said _____ .
(your first name)

"Just be sure to sprinkle some _____
(a gross adjective)

_____ on my food, and add a slice of
(creepy things)

_____ to my _____."
(something gross)   (the disgusting liquid you used above)

(Draw yourself sitting here.)   (Draw your defeated villain lying here.)

86

(Answer on page 125)

HOW TO DRAW
WEDGIE WOMAN

1.   2.   3.   4.

5.   6.

7.   8.

9.   10.

11.

12.

13.

14.

15.

16.

HOW TO DRAW
ZORX, KLAX, AND JENNIFER

1.

2.

3.

4.

5.

6.

7.

8.

9.

10.

11.

12.

13.

14.

15.

16.

91

FUN WITH
ACCESSORIES

1. Add eyelashes!

2. Add lipstick!

3. Add a bow!

ZORXETTE

4a.

4b.

KLAXETTE

5a.

5b.

JENNIFERETTE

6a.

6b.

92

Get ready for the
spine-tingling conclusion of

Hairy Potty

AND   the

UNDERWEAR OF JUSTICE

BY G. R. BEARD and H.M. Hutchins

TreeHouse Comix

INCORPORATED

HAIRY POTTY CHASED OUR HERO outside.

CAPTAIN UNDERPANTS WAS FASTER THAN A Speeding WAISTBAND...

... MORE POWER- FUL THAN BOXER SHORTS...

... And Able to Leap TALL Buildings Without getting A Wedgie.

TRA-LA-LAAAAA!

ZAP

BONK

But Hairy Potty was Powerful, too. He shot an evil Laser Beam at Captain Underpants.

ZAAP

Hey! What's going on here? How come you're not dead?

Never under-estimate the power of underwear!

Finally, CAPTAIN UNDERPANTS And Hairy Potty got into A Big, Terrible Fight.

WARNING

The Following Fight Contains very Graphic violence.

Please cover your eyes when you Turn The pages OR you might get explosive Diarrhea.

—Thank You

FLIP-O-RAMA

HERE's HOW it WORKS !!!!

STEP 1

Place your Left Hand inside the dotted Lines marked "LEFT HAND HERE." Hold the Book open FLAT.

STEP 2

GRASP the Right-hand page with your Right Thumb and index Finger (inside the dotted Lines marked "Right Thumb HERE").

STEP 3

Now Quickly Flip the Right-hand page back and Forth until the picture apears to be animated.

(For extrA fun, try adding your own Sound-effects!)

FLIP-O-RAMA #1

(Pages 99 And 101)

Remember, flip only page 99.
While you are flipping, be sure
You can see the picture on
page 99 And the one on
Page 101.

If you flip quickly,
the two pictures will
Start to look like
One Animated picture.

Left Hand
Here

The Eyeball Basher

RIGHT thumb Here

Right
index
Finger
Here

The EyeBall Basher

FLIP-O-RAMA #2

(pages 103 and 105)

Remember, flip <u>only</u> page 103.
While you are flipping, be sure
you can see the picture on
page 103 <u>And</u> the one on
Page 105.

If you flip Quickly,
the two pictures will
Start to Look Like
<u>One</u> Animated Picture.

Left Hand
Here

THE KOO-KOO CLAP

RIGHT THUMB HERE

Right
index
Finger
Here

104

THE KOO-KOO CLAP

FLIP·O·RAMA #3

(pages 107 and 109)

Remember, flip <u>only</u> page 107.
While you are flipping, be sure
you can see the picture on
page 107 <u>And</u> the one on
Page 109.

If you flip Quickly,
the two pictures will
Start to Look Like
<u>One</u> Animated Picture.

Left Hand
Here

The Potty Pounder

RiGht
Thumb
Here

Right index finger here

108

The Potty Pounder

FLIP-O-RAMA # 4

(pages 111 and 113)

Remember, flip only page 111. While you are flipping, be sure you can see the picture on page 111 And the one on page 113.

If you flip Quickly, the two pictures will start to Look Like One Animated picture.

Left Hand Here

The Psycho Stomp

Right Thumb Here

Right
index
Finger
Here

The Psycho Stomp

ANSWERS

L	U	M	P	Y	U	M	T	E	Y
L	O	O	P	Y	S	I	C	I	K
A	S	Z	A	S	Z	H	R	S	N
B	U	T	T	E	R	C	U	P	I
E	H	S	L	R	J	M	S	O	D
S	Q	U	E	E	Z	I	T	O	G
E	Y	F	F	P	I	H	Y	P	R
E	F	O	A	P	P	C	F	R	E
H	F	O	L	I	P	L	L	A	A
C	U	D	A	K	Y	G	U	H	S
I	L	G	F	S	T	I	N	K	Y
F	F	Y	K	R	O	D	K	V	M
S	N	P	B	L	M	G	Y	D	I
R	E	B	O	O	G	E	R	L	L
P	I	N	K	Y	T	T	O	N	S

Word Find
page 11

Maze
page 14

Crossword
page 17

Word Find
page 21

Crossword
page 39

Word Find
page 41

Maze
page 50

Maze
page 55

Bonus Quiz
page 64

CHART A	CHART B
Benny	Beard
Billy	Fyde
George	Hoskins
Harold	Hutchins
Melvin	Krupp
Morty	Poopypants
Pippy	Ribble
Tara	Sneedly
Tippy	Tinkletrousers

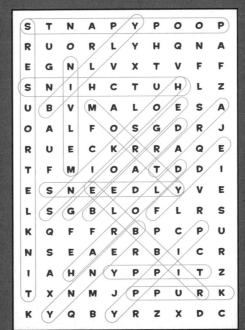

Word Find
page 65

Crossword
page 69

1 Z

3 C O T T O N Y   **4** H
R   A
X   I
R

2 P
5 T O I L E T   **3** C A P T A I   R

O
P
Y
P

6 T
7 L A   **8** D E P U T Y
U
R
B

9 W A I S T B A N D

N   **10** D O G
T   I

11 S U **12** P E **13** R   **14** W O M A N
O   I   P
W   B   E
E   B   **15** S T A R C H
R   L
E

Maze
page 72

Maze
page 87

GET READING W

Dog Man

DAV PILKEY

CREATOR OF CAPTAIN UNDERPANTS

Dog Man UNLEASHED

DAV PILKEY

CREATOR OF CAPTAIN UNDERPANTS

Dog Man A Tale of Two Kitties

DAV PILKEY

CREATOR OF CAPTAIN UNDERPANTS

Dog Man AND CAT KID

DAV PILKEY

CREATOR OF CAPTAIN UNDERPANTS

Dog Man LORD of the FLEAS

DAV PILKEY

CREATOR OF CAPTAIN UNDERPANTS

Dog Man BRAWL of the WILD

DAV PILKEY

CREATOR OF CAPTAIN UNDERPANTS

Dog Man FOR WHOM the BALL ROLLS

DAV PILKEY

CREATOR OF CAPTAIN UNDERPANTS

Dog Man FETCH-22

DAV PILKEY

CREATOR OF CAPTAIN UNDERPANTS

Dog Man GRIME AND PUNISHMENT

DAV PILKEY

CREATOR OF CAPTAIN UNDERPANTS

Dog Man MOTHERING HEIGHTS

DAV PILKEY

CREATOR OF CAPTAIN UNDERPANTS

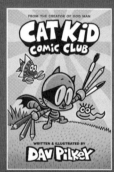

FROM THE CREATOR OF DOG MAN

CAT KID COMIC CLUB

WRITTEN & ILLUSTRATED BY

DAV PILKEY

A GRAPHIC NOVEL FROM THE CREATOR OF DOG MAN

CAT KID COMIC CLUB PERSPECTIVES

WRITTEN & ILLUSTRATED BY

DAV PILKEY

A GRAPHIC NOVEL FROM THE CREATOR OF DOG MAN

CAT KID COMIC CLUB ON PURPOSE

WRITTEN & ILLUSTRATED BY

DAV PILKEY

A GRAPHIC NOVEL FROM THE CREATOR OF DOG MAN

CAT KID COMIC CLUB COLLABORATIONS

WRITTEN & ILLUSTRATED BY

DAV PILKEY

★ "Irreverent, laugh-out-loud funny, and . . . downright moving."
— Publishers Weekly, starred review

ABOUT THE
AUTHOR-ILLUSTRATOR

When Dav Pilkey was a kid, he was diagnosed with ADHD and dyslexia. Dav was so disruptive in class that his teachers made him sit out in the hallway every day. Luckily, Dav loved to draw and make up stories. He spent his time in the hallway creating his own original comic books — the very first adventures of Dog Man and Captain Underpants.

In college, Dav met a teacher who encouraged him to write and illustrate for kids. He took her advice and created his first book, WORLD WAR WON, which won a national competition in 1986. Dav made many other books before being awarded the California Young Reader Medal for DOG BREATH (1994) and the Caldecott Honor for THE PAPERBOY (1996).

In 2002, Dav published his first full-length graphic novel for kids, called THE ADVENTURES OF SUPER DIAPER BABY. It was both a USA Today and New York Times bestseller. Since then, he has published more than a dozen full-length graphic novels for kids, including the bestselling Dog Man and Cat Kid Comic Club series.

Dav's stories are semi-autobiographical and explore universal themes that celebrate friendship, empathy, and the triumph of the good-hearted.

When he is not making books for kids, Dav loves to kayak with his wife in the Pacific Northwest.

Learn more at Pilkey.com.